AF446334

Talisman of Zeus:

A Poetic Tale

Leon X

Author's Note:

I, the author, Leon X, do not promote any of these
actions done through this poetic tale, nor promote
any other actions expressed through any of my works
under Leon X, both in poetics and/or in novels.

Thank you for understanding.

- Leon X

Poetic Tale:

Meet Archeologist Philo. Archeologist Philo finds a
mysterious tale rolled in papyrus hidden inside a
vase covered with black and white ancient paintings.
Astonished by the findings, Philos manages to
translate the works from the ancient language to
modern tone.

He wonders if the Talisman of Zeus was ever real
and if there ever was a character named A'ge'on
through historical texts of that region. Little does
Philo know, what he is to find out about this talisman
and its power, and of the fate of A'ge'on through the
tale.

Yet, the real mystery remains.

Who scribed it?

"Is there not a Talisman within Thy and Thou?"
– Leon X

Archeologist Philo

<u>**1**</u>
Thy am only to translate,
Escribe,
And that is of all,
And of nothing else.

A'ge'on

<u>**1**</u>
Is not the Olympus Mount of thine?
And thine a'lone?
Am Thy not the Sun of Zeus?
Of the Sun?

<u>**2**</u>
And the Creator of Gods?
Or of His Son?
O'
Zeus!

<u>3</u>
Cast down Thou lighting,
Let Thy charge wunce more,
And once more again...
Is it not of Thy?

<u>**4**</u>
The Creator of Olympus?
The maker of lands?
And of cities?
And of those un'der Thy kin?

<u>5</u>
Or is it of the o'ther?
Is there any other above Thy?
There be not,
Am Thy not of the Mount of Olympus?

<u>6</u>
Is it not Thy abode?
Upon these lands of Gods, Goddesses and of
Demi'Gods,
Am Thy not of the finest?
Fiercest?

<u>7</u>
Strongest?
And of the Sun?
Sun of All,
Is it not Thy light that shineth upon thee?

<u>**8**</u>
Or is it of the else?
Am Thy not of the truth?
And is this not through Thy and Thy a'lone?
It is Thy strength...

<u>9</u>
Over the lands,
Do not mortals pray'th to Thy and Thy a'lone?
Upon Thy Mount,
Thy name'd of Olympus?

<u>**10**</u>
Or am Thy only a Sun,
The Sun,
The Sun of Zeus,
The Almighty,

<u>**11**</u>

Are not lightning signs of heat?
Heat un'to light?
And light un'to ground?
Is it not Thy wish and wisheth a'lone?

<u>12</u>

Or it is of the Father?
Whom is of greater?
The Mount?
Or Thy?

<u>13</u>
Of Thy Father?
Or of Thy Sun?
Is it not Thy and Thy a'lone?
Whom grant'th boons and of gifts?

<u>**14**</u>
Or is it of the o'ther?
Am Thy not of the God of Olympus?
The Creator of Demi'Gods?
Are they not of Thy seed and seed a'lone?

<u>15</u>
As Thy lay atop Thy abode,
Over the lands,
Whom are all influence'd by Thy and Thy a'lone?
Are not temples in Thy name?

<u>**16**</u>

Are not Thy rivaled by elements and elements
a'lone?
Is it not Thy and Thy a'lone whom is of Thunder?
And of Lightning?
Heat?

<u>17</u>

And of strength of a thousand bulls?
The maker of men from dirt and of breath?
Bow down to Thy at Thy temples,
Am Thy not the Sun?

<u>**18**</u>

And is not the Sun of Thy?
Am Thy not of the Sun?
And the Sun of Thy?
Over the Mount of Thy a'bode,

<u>**19**</u>
And a'bode a'lone...
In silence...
So it is to be...
Whose Mount is it?

<u>**20**</u>
Thy and Thy a'lone?
Or of the o'ther?
Whom casted me to a Demi'God?
Was it not Thyself?

<u>21</u>
Or from the anointment of the Great?
Beyond Thy?
Or of Zeus Himself?
If Thy am of Zeus,

<u>**22**</u>

Is not His Mount?
So it be'th?
Thy am the envy of the Gods,
And Gods a'lone...

<u>**23**</u>

Shall Apollo escribe poems of Thy?
Shall He?
Am Thy not of Zeus?
The Creator of Nation and influence thereon,

<u>**24**</u>

The strength of thousand warriors on a battlefield
against giants,
Is it not of Thy?
It is of Thy,
Thy am of the roaring Sun,

<u>25</u>

And of Zeus,

The O'lympian Zeus himself,

Is it not Thy bloodline whom will be'th of royalty?

And of royalty a'lone?

<u>**26**</u>

Is not this Talisman of Zeus?
The God of Gods of these lands?
Am Thy not of his kin?
As His blood floweth through Thy and Thy a'lone,

<u>**27**</u>

Am Thy not of the chosen?
The man whom be'th of stone to liveth forever?
And to be worshipped within towns, cities and of
acropolises?
Is it not of Thy?

<u>28</u>

The Ever-Glowing Sun?
The Talisman Holder of the Great God Himself?
The envy of the Gods of Greek,
Over the Mounts of this land?

<u>29</u>
Was it not Thy whom hath kept Thy eye on the
Spartans?
And Spartans a'lone?
Bow down to Thy,
For Thy am of the One,

<u>**30**</u>
The One,
The Blood of the Titans,
And Creator of They,
And They a'lone,

<u>**31**</u>
Air,
Light,
Atmosphere,
Space of the invisible without harm,

<u>32</u>
Hera,
Apollo,
Ares,
Artemis,

<u>**33**</u>

Dionysus,

Hermes,

Apollo,

Athena,

<u>34</u>
Hephaestus?
Am Thy not of the Creator of All?
Does not Thy Talisman giveth Thy strength and
powers both in the seen and of the un'seen?
Through the God bless'd by Saturn himself,

<u>35</u>
Un'rivaled,
Un'matched,
Un'fathomable to mortal mind,
To govern all?

<u>36</u>
Upon all lands?
Am Thy not of the Sun?!
O'
Ancient waters of love and of hate whom form seas,

<u>**37**</u>
Thy am to drinketh,
Do Thy not need of both to liveth?
Or am Thy to liveth in im'balance?
With Thy Talisman whilst liveth in the forests
a'lone?

<u>**38**</u>

So women of olde could crafteth tales,
Of horror to their children?
May they be of right?
Since Thy am of the Talisman of the Utmost and of
the Supreme?

<u>39</u>
Since Thy am of the power,
Is it not Thy to control and wield'th and wield'th
a'lone?
And none other are to cometh near nor taketh,
Un'til Thy death,

<u>40</u>

Or if Thy am to purposefully giveth to an'other,
Whom Thy am to trusteth in,
Yet...
That is of nowhere neareth to cometh,

<u>**41**</u>
Am Thy not of the POWERFUL?!
The Sun of Zeus!
The embodiment of His Grace and of His Power...
Over the Mount that is soon to be of thine,

<u>**42**</u>
And thine a'lone,
Are not the Gods envious of Thy?
And Thy a'lone?
As Thy am only to taketh what Thy desireth,

<u>43</u>
And to curseth what Thy hate,
Am Thy not the Creator of Order as columns
hold'th up temples?
Is there not supposed to be of a ruler?
One?

<u>**44**</u>
A One?
The God?
God of Gods?
God of the Demi'Gods?

<u>45</u>
And spirits of Nature?
Or am Thy of only to follow?
And only of a Man,
With the source in Thy hand,

<u>**46**</u>

A Talisman of red surrounded by blue gem crested
in fine gold,
Only to be of kept by the sacred,
Within and without,
Through Thy a'lone...

<u>**47**</u>

Am Thy not the God of Olympus?
The God whom crea'th lands?
Am Thy not of the lover of Queen Hera?
Am Thy not of the Oak?

<u>**48**</u>

Am Thy not of the eagle?
Am Thy not in the sky and of the Mount?
Am Thy not the Sun of the Maker?
Am Thy not of the line of lightning whom scars the
night sky?

<u>49</u>

Am Thy not of the bull of power and of sexual
vi'gor?
Am Thy not of the strong?
Am Thy not of the order?
Am Thy not of the civil?

<u>50</u>
Am Thy not of strength?
Am Thy not of the wise?
Am Thy not the one lover whom is of a Queen?
Am Thy not of the power and power a'lone?

<u>**51**</u>
And of now,
Thy am to rest...
As Thy Talisman is of me and Thy am of it,
Rest...

<u>**52**</u>
Where is it...
The caduceus of Hermes?
May it be use'd for Thy sleep...
Sleep...

<u>53</u>
Whom is this whom hath disturb'th Thy sleep?
Am Thy not the maker and ruler of the Mount?!
How dare'th this mongrel even cometh close to
Thy?!
What?!

<u>54</u>
HELP!
THIS BE A MAN OF BUTCHERY!
HELP!
HELP!

Mysterious Man

<u>1</u>
The Talisman of Zeus,
Is within and without,
And now it is with Thy,
And Thy a'lone...

<u>**2**</u>
Is it not now,
Thy whom is of the Power?
The Power,
Of Zeus?

End.

About the Author

Leon X is a novelist and poet.

Visit www.leonxtheauthor.com for more information on
the author.

Thank you for supporting.